"'VAN GOOL'S'"

White Fang

SMITHMARK

Chapter 1
THE WILD NORTH

The most northern part of Alaska, in the United States, is a wild, savage country. Winters are very hard and last for nine months of the year. During winter the days are very short and the sun hardly shines at all. It gets so cold that the rivers freeze over, and those hunters brave enough to go out in the harsh conditions use them as roads. Only the toughest hunters venture out to hunt the wild lynx, bear and deer. Their dogs, too, need to be strong and hardy to survive in this wilderness.

Many years ago, in the time when this story took place, hardly anyone lived out in the wild north. However, the American Indians often set up their winter camps in the forests, putting up their teepees around great fires. These fires protected them from the cold, but also from the wolves.

For there were a great many wolves in the wild, and they often followed the hunters waiting for a chance to attack. Men were always on the watch, in case a wolf attacked the dogs, or even the hunters themselves! But the wolves were not cruel, they simply needed food to survive in such a harsh country. One Spring an old wolf set out to hunt for food for his family. His coat was grey, and he was covered in old hunting and fighting scars. The she-wolf was sheltering under some rocks with her young cubs. They had not found food for many days, but this time they were lucky, for the old wolf caught a rabbit.

The old wolf was very proud of his fine family. However, as the five cubs were still young, their mother could not leave them. It was up to the old wolf alone to go hunting. Every day he would roam far and wide in search of food, and at first he always managed to catch something. But for many days now he had returned with nothing except new scratches and bites. As the days passed the wolf cubs grew thin and weak, and soon four of them had died. The remaining cub had always been the strongest; livelier and more intelligent than the others. Finally there came a day when the old wolf did not return to the cave. The she-wolf knew that something terrible must have happened to him.

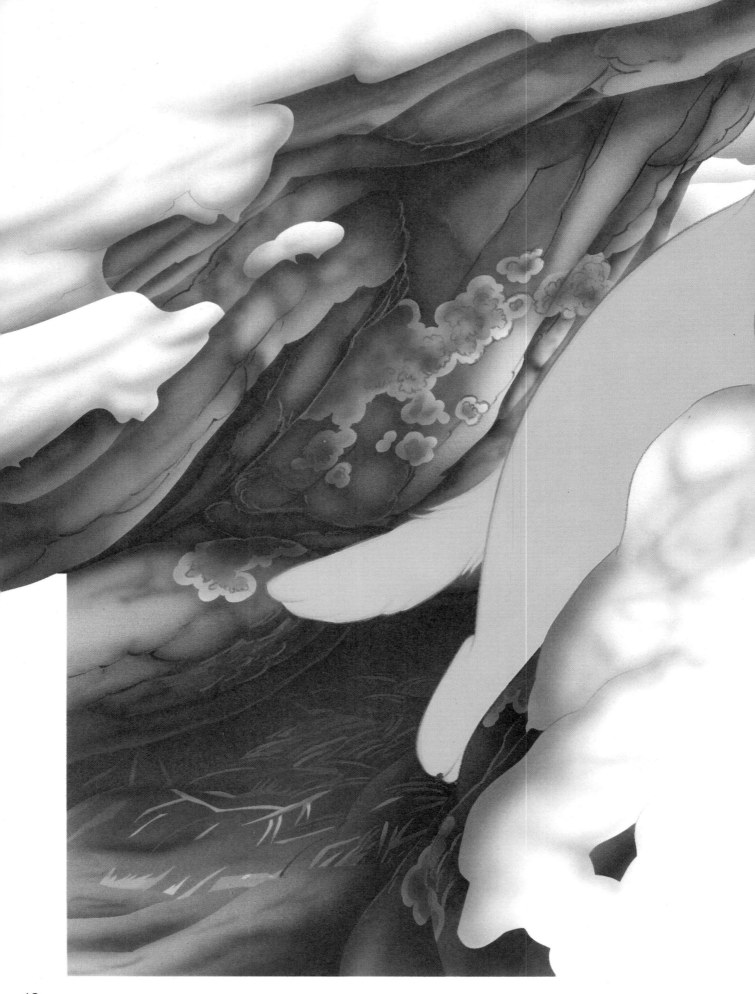

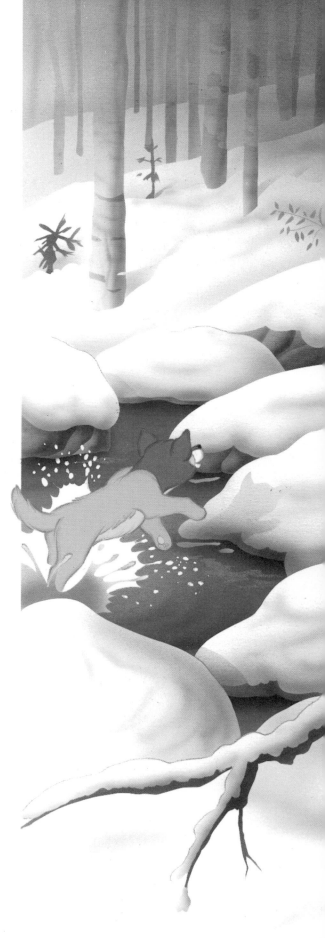

The old wolf had finally met his match in a fight. He had been killed by a lynx, half mad with hunger. A few days later the she-wolf found the spot where the two had fought, and she knew that the old wolf would not return. Now she had to hunt for food for her cub. Each day she left him alone in the cave.

For many days he stayed inside, scared of the world outside, but one day he grew bolder and scrambled out of the cave, sniffing the cool fresh air. There were hundreds of new smells, and excitedly he ran and rolled in the snow. Suddenly he saw something sparkling through the trees. It was the river. The ice had melted, and the water was swirling and flooding along the banks. Not realising the danger, the wolf cub leaped into the river. At once his nose filled with icy water, and the current pulled him along. With a surge of strength he managed to fight his way to the bank, where he lay, panting for breath, but very proud of himself!

Over the next few days the cub explored the forest. He learned to find food for himself, catching small animals and birds. He was not cruel, but he knew the tough law of the wild – eat or be eaten. One day he was nearly killed himself. He had backed a weasel up to a tree when the animal suddenly leaped for his throat. The cub was only saved when his mother returned from hunting just in time. He learned the hard way that although weasels are small, they are one of the most ferocious animals in the forest.

A few days later he came to his mother's rescue. As she returned to the cave, she was suddenly attacked by the lynx that had killed the old wolf! The young cub heard her snarls, and ran through the trees. Without hesitating he leaped on to the lynx's back. The lynx was taken by surprise, and the she-wolf managed to win the fight.

Chapter 2
GREY BEAVER

Every day the wolf cub roamed further from the cave. One morning as he came into a clearing, he stopped in astonishment. Five strange animals came towards him, walking on two legs! Although they did not attack or threaten him, the cub could not move for terror. These men were a group of hunters from the nearby Indian camp. Just then his mother came rushing into the clearing, growling fiercely! He ran to her and hid between her paws. "Kiche!" exclaimed one of the men. To the cub's surprise his mother immediately lay down on the ground before the men, wagging her tail. He knew then that these creatures must be very powerful if they could make the fierce she-wolf obey them.

One of the Indians, Grey Beaver, had recognised the she-wolf, for she had been brought up in the camp. Several years ago there had been a terrible famine, and she had left the Indians. She had preferred to take her chances in the forest, where she had met the old scarred wolf. "So, this is your son," said Grey Beaver, reaching out to pet the cub, who bared his teeth. "He's a fierce one!" he laughed. "What strong white teeth he has. We must call him White Fang!"

The Indians began to make their way back to the camp. Grey Beaver called to Kiche, who followed him at once. White Fang trailed along behind. That evening when the Indians lit their great fire the flames fascinated him. He poked his nose into the fire then ran away, howling in pain, mocking laughter ringing in his ears.

White Fang was surprised at the size of the Indian camp. Dozens of teepees were spread all along the river bank. He trotted around the camp, curious to learn about everything. The camp children seemed friendly, but often threw stones at the dogs, so White Fang learned to stay out of their way. He soon understood that the women were often cross and shouted, but they nearly always had a bone or treat for him. Most importantly, White Fang learned to respect the men, for they ruled the camp.

The other dogs were very jealous of White Fang, and never missed a chance to bite or snap at him. His worst enemy was Lip-Lip, a dog his own age. One day Lip-Lip was chasing White Fang when he ran straight into the she-wolf. She growled so fiercely at the little dog that he stayed away from White Fang for many days afterwards!

So White Fang grew used to life in the Indian camp. But one day his world was turned upside down for he was separated from his mother. Grey Beaver gave Kiche to Three Eagles, the chief of a neighbouring tribe. When White Fang saw the she-wolf getting into the canoe with her new master, he tried to leap into the river after her. Grey Beaver caught hold of him, but the wolf cub was so determined to get away that he bit the Indian. "Wretched animal!" cried Grey Beaver, "I'm going to teach you a lesson!" He beat poor White Fang until he lay half senseless on the river bank. Lip-Lip sneaked up to the wolf-cub, but before he had a chance to attack, Grey Beaver chased him away. And so White Fang learned another lesson – that the Indian was a harsh master, but a fair one.

Chapter 3
LEARNING TO HATE

Although he missed his mother, White Fang soon learned to survive on his own. He knew that Grey Beaver would protect him if he were in danger, but he also knew that the Indian would never pet him or show him any love. He had no friends among the other camp dogs either. They were wary of him, and he had to fight them all before they learned to respect him. His upbringing in the harsh northern wilderness had made him strong and cunning. In a fight he knew to leap straight for the throat, which is an animal's weakest spot. But he also knew to run away if attacked by a stronger animal. This was the valuable lesson Grey Beaver had taught him – to always respect someone stronger than you, but to make those weaker respect you.

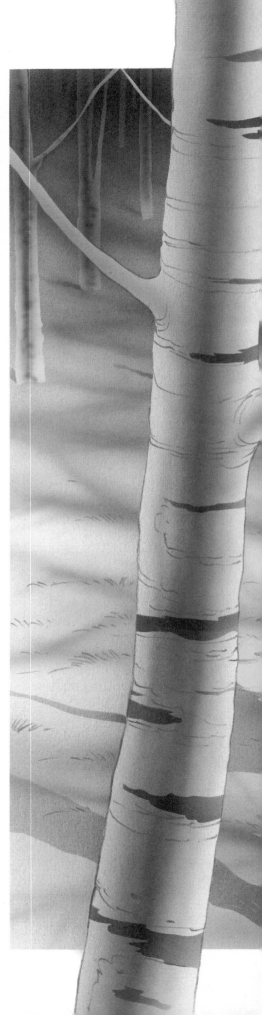

When Autumn came, Grey Beaver decided to move south, where the winter would not be so harsh. The whole camp was on the move, and everyone bustled around, taking down the tents and packing up all their belongings. For many months White Fang had been dreaming of returning to the wild. When he saw all the confusion in the camp, he decided to slip away into the forest. But when night fell he was afraid and hungry. After living in the Indian camp for so long, White Fang had forgotten how to live in the wild! He hurried back to the camp but when he got there everyone had gone!

For two long days he followed the Indians' trail. Suddenly, through the trees, he saw the light of a fire. As he got closer he recognised Grey Beaver. Slowly he crept up to his master, expecting a beating for running away. But to his surprise, Grey Beaver was delighted to see him! "White Fang!" cried the Indian. "You've found us! Well done!" And he threw the wolf cub a tender piece of meat.

White Fang knew that he could never go back to the wild and was glad to stay with his master. But although he felt he belonged in the camp, he was still a wolf, and the other dogs never stopped hating him. The years passed, and White Fang grew into a great strong wolf. Grey Beaver decided that it was time to train him to pull one of the sleds. He placed White Fang at the head of the team, and no sled ever moved so fast! For the dogs were all trying to catch White Fang, and he was careful to keep ahead of them. At first he had tried to turn round and fight them, but Grey Beaver whipped him until he learned to run instead. Grey Beaver was very proud of White Fang. "He is a fierce wolf," he would say. "But he always obeys me!"

One summer, the Indians travelled down the river to Fort Yukon, a large town. Throughout the winter Grey Beaver had collected a great pile of furs and made them into coats and hats. The people of Fort Yukon were rich, and paid well for these furs.

White Fang had never seen such people, and learned that they were even more powerful than the Indians. For these were rich Americans, who had made their money when gold was discovered in Alaska. They could buy anything they wanted, lived in fine houses and wore expensive clothes. There were many of them, more people than White Fang had seen in his whole life. More of them arrived every day, eager to make their fortune in gold.

Chapter 4
BEAUTY SMITH

As he grew used to the town, White Fang noticed that all
the men had at least one dog. But what poor animals they
were! They would run yipping to their masters if he bit
them. Grey Beaver was busy selling his furs, and had little
time for White Fang, so the wolf spent his days terrorising
the local dogs. There was a man in town who seemed to
enjoy watching the dogs fight, and he would often watch
White Fang. "Go on!" he'd yell, "Bite him. You're not
scared are you?" And White Fang would be so angry that
he would fight even more fiercely. This man was known as
Beauty Smith. In fact he was no beauty – he was very
ugly, and was mean and cruel.

White Fang did not know that Beauty Smith kept trying to buy him from Grey Beaver. At first the Indian refused to sell, although Beauty Smith was offering him a large sum of money. But one night Beauty Smith took Grey Beaver to the inn, and got him so drunk on whisky that Grey Beaver sold White Fang for almost nothing!

White Fang tried to escape, but Beauty Smith kept him chained up. Everyone in the town came to see the wolf, and teased and poked fun at him until he become wild with rage. Then Beauty Smith had an idea. He organised fights between the wolf and the town dogs. Men would come and place bets with Beauty Smith that their dog would win. White Fang always won, and Beauty Smith collected a pile of money every evening. Although it was White Fang who won him the money, Beauty Smith treated him cruelly.

Within several weeks there were no more dogs left for White Fang to fight. Beauty Smith decided to go to another town. He kept the poor wolf in a tiny cage, only letting him out to fight. White Fang had become so fierce that he killed all the dogs brought to fight him. Then one day a new dog arrived, a bulldog, with a ferocious reputation. As soon as the fight began, he leaped at White Fang, and knocked him to the ground! The crowd went wild, and the bets became even larger. "Get up!" cried Beauty Smith, "Kill him!" But every time White Fang tried to go in for the kill, the bulldog fought free. At last he forced White Fang to the ground, and began to bite him savagely. Beauty Smith was furious and began to kick and beat the wolf. He was so angry he wanted to kill him. Suddenly a voice rang out, "Leave him alone, you brute!"

Chapter 5
MR SCOTT

The man who had called out stepped forward, and Beauty Smith stood away from White Fang. "It's Mr Scott," whispered the men in the crowd. "He owns the mine. He can get you fired if you're not careful." Although Beauty Smith was impressed, the bulldog was not. He was still biting White Fang, who lay still. Scott called for his dog handler. "Matt, get them apart." Matt used his revolver to prise open the bulldog's jaws, and pulled the two animals apart. The bulldog's owner was angry, but dared not say anything against Mr Scott. "I'll buy this dog from you," said Scott to Beauty Smith. Beauty Smith was sure that White Fang was dead, and took the money without a complaint.

Mr Scott and Matt looked after White Fang, and within a few weeks he was strong and well once more. But he was even more vicious than before, and Scott had to keep him chained up. "He is a wolf, after all," sighed Scott. "We cannot expect anything else."

One day Matt noticed that White Fang's fur was marked where he had worn a harness. "Look," he said to Mr Scott, "Someone has already tamed him." Mr Scott realised that White Fang was savage because of the ill-treatment he had received from Beauty Smith.

As the weeks passed White Fang began to trust him, and grew gradually less fierce. Unluckily, one day when Mr Scott brought him his dinner, one of the other dogs ran up and snatched the meat. At once White Fang attacked, and before Scott could stop him, he had killed the dog! Matt wanted to shoot him, but Scott shook his head. "He doesn't know any other way to behave," he said sadly. "It is not his fault!"

Instead of punishing White Fang, Mr Scott continued to treat him kindly. Every day he gently stroked the wolf, who growled for he did not understand kindness anymore. Then one day he realised that Mr Scott meant him no harm, and began to enjoy being cared for. Mr Scott and Matt were delighted, and soon White Fang was tamed again. Once more he pulled a sled, and every evening he would sit close to his new master.

One evening when he returned with Matt, Mr Scott was nowhere to be seen. "He's gone to town on business," Matt told him. But White Fang was miserable. He didn't understand that Mr Scott would be coming back. He wouldn't eat, and Matt began to worry about him. At last Scott returned home. White Fang watched him for a moment, then leaped up and began licking his face. Mr Scott was delighted!

Chapter 6
LEARNING TO LOVE

A few months later, Mr Scott had to go away again. "Look at him," said Matt, pointing to White Fang. "He knows you're leaving and he won't eat anything." Mr Scott was sorry to leave White Fang, but what could he do? "I can't take him with me to California, Matt!" he said. His home was in San Francisco, but he hated the idea of leaving White Fang behind. On the day Scott was leaving, Matt had to shut White Fang in the barn, where he howled miserably. All the way to the dock, Mr Scott thought about White Fang. Sadly he boarded the boat, and walked up to the deck. As he looked down at the gangway, his eyes widened in surprise – for there was White Fang! The wolf was looking at him pleadingly. "OK, you win," murmured Scott, and brought White Fang on board. The wolf had been so determined to join his master that he had broken out of the barn!

When White Fang got off the boat in San
Francisco, he was terrified. Never had he seen so
many people! The city was huge. The streets were so
long he could not see the end, and the buildings
were so tall that they shut out the sky! Worst of all
were the motor cars that rushed past. They smelled
terrible, and the noise of their engines was
frightening. He trembled with fear as Mr Scott
climbed into one of the machines. But White Fang
trusted his master and followed him into the car,
where he lay at his feet.

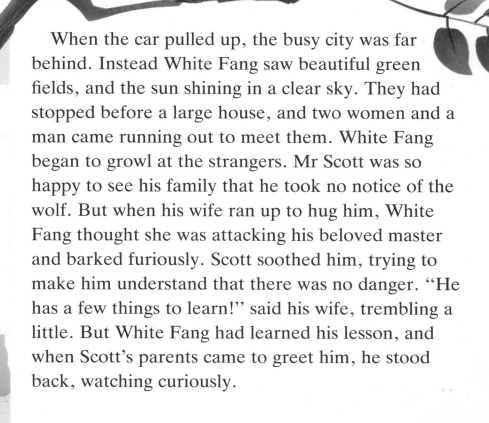

When the car pulled up, the busy city was far behind. Instead White Fang saw beautiful green fields, and the sun shining in a clear sky. They had stopped before a large house, and two women and a man came running out to meet them. White Fang began to growl at the strangers. Mr Scott was so happy to see his family that he took no notice of the wolf. But when his wife ran up to hug him, White Fang thought she was attacking his beloved master and barked furiously. Scott soothed him, trying to make him understand that there was no danger. "He has a few things to learn!" said his wife, trembling a little. But White Fang had learned his lesson, and when Scott's parents came to greet him, he stood back, watching curiously.

There was worse to come. For suddenly another dog came racing out of the house and jumped up to greet Mr Scott! Furious, White Fang turned on the dog who was trying to take his master away. But just as he was about to attack he suddenly stopped. For the dog was female, and all White Fang's instincts told him that he must not attack her. Instead he contented himself with growling jealously whenever she came near Mr Scott. "This is Collie," said Mr Scott, "And here's Dick!" Dick was Mr Scott's terrier, and White Fang soon learned to respect him.

As the weeks passed, White Fang great used to living in the great house. He was never violent, but he was never friendly either. The servants, the other dogs and even Scott's wife and children tried to make friends with him, but White Fang simply ignored them. The only friend he wanted was Mr Scott.

However, White Fang was not completely tamed. Every day he would walk past the hen house, licking his lips hungrily. One day the servant forgot the close the henhouse door, and at once White Fang leaped inside. He attacked the poor chickens and they flapped around, squawking in terror. Luckily Collie came past, and when she saw what was happening she leaped at White Fang. Not daring to attack her, he ran off back to the house. When Mr Scott heard about the attack, he was not angry. Instead he took White Fang to the henhouse every day, and taught him to leave the chickens alone. White Fang learned his lesson well. Whenever he heard his master cry, "Down!" he would lay on the ground obediently. He never touched another chicken!

Slowly White Fang learned to behave. He knew he was allowed to hunt and chase wild animals, but the farm and household animals were forbidden. He understood that he must not attack children, even when they threw stones at him. White Fang found this particularly hard to bear, especially when one day in town a boy hit him with a very large stone. But to his surprise, Mr Scott caught the boy and beat him. At last White Fang understood that he was cared for. He began to love Mr Scott's family too, and his children, Maud and Weedon, became his great friends. Only Collie continued to treat him coldly.

Mr Scott would often go out riding in the woods and White Fang always went with him. One morning the horse was startled by a fox and reared up. She lost her balance and fell to the ground, throwing Mr Scott from her back. Scott groaned with pain, but could not stand up. White Fang tried to pull him to his feet, but Scott managed to whisper, "Leave me, go to the house and fetch help." White Fang raced back to the house, and found Mrs Scott in the kitchen. He stopped before her, looking at her, then looking back towards the woods. Suddenly she realised something was wrong. "Where is your master?" she cried. White Fang howled, then turned and began running back towards the trees. Mrs Scott called to the servants, and they followed the faithful wolf.

The horse quickly recovered, but Mr Scott spent several weeks in bed. White Fang would not leave his side until he was up and about. The wolf's love and loyalty had won over everyone in the house. "That animal's getting more and more like a dog every day!" smiled Mrs Scott. But most surprisingly, Collie began to look at White Fang in a different way. They could often be seen together, walking through the trees outside, or laying side by side on the hearth. It seemed that the wild wolf had won the heart of the haughty Collie!

The following Spring, Collie gave birth to six beautiful puppies. They all looked like their mother, except one, who had a shaggy grey coat like a wolf! He was lively and intelligent, and when he was old enough to leave his mother, he would follow White Fang around everywhere! Mr Scott and his wife laughed to see White Fang and his family playing together, and Mr Scott was always glad that he had saved the wolf from his savage life.